MY WORLD in GERMAN

Coloring Book & Picture Dictionary

Tamara M. Mealer

National Textbook Company
a division of *NTC Publishing Group* • Lincolnwood, Illinois USA

To Parents and Teachers

Research has shown that the best way to help children learn a language is to involve them physically in the learning process. Entertaining, hands-on activities engage children's enthusiasm and encourage greater retention of learning.

My World in German has been created for today's young learner of German with these findings in mind. The coloring pages spark children's interest and involve them in hands-on activities. As they color, children will notice that some people or items in the pictures are numbered. They can look up the names of these people in German and English on the page opposite the picture. A pronunciation guide follows each German word to promote correct pronunciation. When the pictures have been colored, *My World in German* becomes a delightful picture dictionary that children have helped create themselves.

Each picture is also accompanied by a few questions designed to help children practice the words they are learning and encourage them to use the German names of items in the pictures. Use the questions as a guide for formulating more questions about the pictures and for starting conversations about the German words presented in each one. The more involved you become in a child's language-learning process, the more she or he will learn.

1996 Printing

Published by National Textbook Company, a division of NTC Publishing Group.
© 1992 by NTC Publishing Group, 4255 West Touhy Avenue,
Lincolnwood (Chicago), Illinois 60646-1975 U.S.A.

About This Book

This book will help you learn to talk about your world in German. You will find pictures of places you know, like the classroom, the kitchen, the beach, the zoo, the circus, and many more. Color the pictures any way you like!

While you are coloring, you will notice numbers next to some of the objects or people in the picture. Look at the same numbers on the page across from the picture. You will find the names of the people and objects next to the numbers. First, you will see the names in German. After each German word, you will see a pronunciation guide in parentheses. This tells you how to say the German word out loud. It may look funny, but if you read it out loud, you will be saying the word correctly. To find out more about how to say sounds in German and using the pronunciation guides, read the section called "How to Say German Sounds." Lastly, you will also find the name of each person or object in English.

The pages across from the pictures also have some questions about what you see in each picture. Try to answer the questions with the German words you have learned. The answers to the questions are in an answer key at the back of the book, but don't peek until you have tried to answer the questions yourself!

At the beginning of the book, there are some facts about the German language. Knowing these will help you when you use the words you have learned to talk about things in German.

Share this book with your parents or with your friends. Learning German is a lot of fun, but you will enjoy it even more if you do it with a friend. *Viel Spaß!* (Have fun!)

Contents

To Parents and Teachers
About This Book
Some Helpful Hints about German
How to Say German Sounds
Using the Guide to Saying Words
More Useful Words in German

1. **Unser Haus** / Our House
2. **Das Wohnzimmer** / The Living Room
3. **Die Küche** / The Kitchen
4. **Das Klassenzimmer** / The Classroom
5. **Die Kleidung** / Clothing
6. **Die Jahreszeiten und das Wetter** / The Seasons and the Weather
7. **Der Sport** / Sports
8. **Die Stadt** / The City
9. **Der Supermarkt** / The Supermarket
10. **Im Restaurant** / In the Restaurant
11. **Das Postamt** / The Post Office
12. **Die Bank** / The Bank
13. **Beim Arzt** / At the Doctor's Office
14. **Die Tankstelle** / The Service Station
15. **Die Verkehrsmittel** / Transportation
16. **Der Bauernhof** / The Farm
17. **Die Tiere im Zoo** / Animals in the Zoo
18. **Am Strand** / At the Beach
19. **Der Zirkus** / The Circus
20. **Die Musikinstrumente** / Musical Instruments
21. **Die Tätigkeitswörter** / Action Words
22. **Die Zahlen** / Numbers
23. **Die Formen** / Shapes
24. Color the Shapes
25. Draw Your Own Picture
    Antworten auf die Fragen / Answers to the Questions

Some Helpful Hints about German

Masculine, Feminine, and Neuter Words

In German, all nouns (people, places, and things) are either masculine, feminine, or neuter. Words that have the word **der** before them are masculine. For example, **der Fisch** (the fish) is masculine. Words with **die** before them are feminine, so **die Blume** (the flower) is feminine. Words that have the word **das** before them are neuter, neither masculine nor feminine. Therefore, **das Haus** (the house) is neuter. **Der, die,** and **das** all mean "the" in German. They are usually used when you talk about people, places, and things.

Talking about More Than One

When you want to talk about more than one of something, you sometimes must add an **e** or an **en** to the end of a word. Sometimes you don't have to add anything. These are things you will learn by heart as you learn to speak German.

Masculine, feminine, and neuter nouns all use the German word **die** to show there is more than one. So, for example, more than one fish is **die Fische,** more than one flower is **die Blumen,** and more than one house is **die Häuser.**

How to Say German Sounds

In German, many letters are said in a different way from English. The best way to learn to say German sounds is to listen to German-speaking people and copy what they say. Germans say the letters *C, F, H, K, M, N, P,* and *T* the same as in English. We have given you some rules to help you with the other letters. German also has four more letters than the English alphabet. These are: **ä, ö, ü,** and **ß.**

Below is a list of letters, with a guide to show you how to say each one. For each German sound, there is an English word (or part of a word) that sounds like it. Read it out loud to find out how to say the German sound. Then, practice saying the examples of each sound.

Vowels

Letter(s)		English	German
a	long	*f*a*ther*	Gas
a	short	*c*a*rt*	Monat
ä	long	*m*a*ze*	Käse
ä	short	*l*e*t*	Äpfel
au		*n*ow	Sau
äu		*t*oy	Bräu
e	long	*c*a*ke*	Dresden
e	short	*l*e*t*	der
ei		*h*i*gh*	Kleid
er		*air*	Erde
eu		*b*oy	Feuer
i	long	*s*ee	Stil
i	short	*b*i*t*	Tirol
ie		*s*ee	Kiefer
ir		*f*ear	Birke
o	long	*g*o	Boden
o	short	o*bey*	Auto
ö		Say *o* and push your lips forward.	Öl
u	long	*d*o	Buch
u	short	*p*u*ll*	Purpur
ü		Say *u* and push your lips forward, as if to say "few."	Kostüm

Consonants

b	u*p*	Abfall
d	dar*t*	Kleid
g	*g*irl	Tiger
g	Sometimes sounds like "gara*g*e."	Genie
j	*y*ard	Jäger
l	The tip of your tongue touches the front of your mouth very lightly.	Laden
pf	Say both sounds together.	Pfeffer
q	*kv*etch	Qualität
r	Say this sound at the back of your throat, a little like gargling.	Ratte
s	slipper*s*	Salz
v	*f*ather	Vater
w	*v*ase	Wasser
x	so*cks*	Xylophon
z	ra*ts*	Zug
ß	*s*oup	Straße
ch	Sometimes sounds like this: Shape your mouth as if to make the *ee* sound and blow through it. It sounds a little like *sh*.	Milch
	Sometimes sounds like this: Say *k,* as in du*k*e, but don't let your tongue touch the roof of your mouth; blow through it.	Nacht

Using the Guide to Saying Words

After each German word in this book, you will find a pronunciation guide in parentheses. This is a special spelling that tells you how to say the word correctly. It may look funny, but if you read the pronunciation guide out loud, you will be saying the word correctly.

In the pronunciation guides, we've given special spellings for sounds that are not found in English. The German *r* (R in the pronunciation guides) has a sound that is not found in English. Say this sound at the back of your throat, a little like gargling. When you see *OE* in the pronunciation guides, say the sound by shaping your lips as if to say the *oh* sound and holding your tongue as if to make the *ay* sound. To make the *H* sound, shape your mouth to make the *ee* sound and blow through it. It should sound a little like *sh,* but much lighter. To make the *K* sound, say *k,* as in *duke,* but don't let your tongue touch the roof of your mouth; blow through it.

Here are a few more hints for using the pronunciation guides. Always pronounce *ow* like the *ow* in *now.* Always pronounce *igh* like the *i* in *night. Ah* always sounds like the *a* in *father* and *oh* always sounds like the *o* in *go.*

You should also remember that every word has a stressed syllable. This is the syllable that must be said a little louder than the others. In the pronunciation guides, the stressed syllable is in bold letters. In German, the first syllable is usually stressed, so most of the time, you will say the first syllable of a word a little louder than the others. But when German has borrowed words from other languages, the stress will change, so watch carefully.

More Useful Words in German

Here are a few useful words that are not included in the pictures.

Die Wochentage	Days of the Week
Montag (**mohn**-tahg)	Monday
Dienstag (**deens**-tahg)	Tuesday
Mittwoch (**mit**-voH)	Wednesday
Donnerstag (**dohn**-naiRs-stahg)	Thursday
Freitag (**frigh**-tahg)	Friday
Samstag / Sonnabend (**zahmz**-tahg / **zohn**-ahp-pent)	Saturday
Sonntag (**zohn**-tahg)	Sunday

Die Monate des Jahres	Months of the Year
Januar (**yahn**-oo-ahR)	January
Februar (**fayp**-Roo-ahR)	February
März (mayRts)	March
April (ah-**pRil**)	April
Mai (migh)	May
Juni (**yoo**-nee)	June
Juli (**yoo**-lee)	July
August (**owg**-goost)	August
September (zept-**tem**-baiR)	September
Oktober (ohk-**toh**-baiR)	October
November (noh-**fem**-baiR)	November
Dezember (day-**tsem**-baiR)	December

1. Unser Haus (oon-zaiR hows)   Our House

1. **die Berge** (dee **baiR**-guh)   mountains
2. **die Bäume** (dee **boy**-muh)   trees
3. **die Mauer** (dee **mow**-eR)   (garden) wall
4. **die Kiefer** (dee **kee**-faiR)   pine tree
5. **die Garage** (dee guh-**Rah**-zhe)   garage
6. **der Stein** (daiR shtighn)   stone
7. **das Schwimmbad** (dahs **shvimm**-bahd)   swimming pool
8. **die Forke** (dee **fohR**-kuh)   gardening fork
9. **die Blumenkelle** (dee **bloo**-men-kel-luh)   gardening shovel
10. **das Loch** (dahs lawK)   hole
11. **die Erde** (dee **aiR**-duh)   soil
12. **der Briefkasten** (daiR **bReef**-kah-sten)   mailbox
13. **der Schubkarren** (daiR **shoop**-kahR-Ren)   wheelbarrow

14. **die Blumen** (dee **bloo**-men)   flowers
15. **die Blätter** (dee **blet**-taiR)   leaves
16. **der Zweig** (daiR tsvighg)   tree branch
17. **die Hundehütte** (dee **hoon**-de-heut-te)   doghouse
18. **der Hund** (daiR hoont)   dog
19. **der Gärtner** (daiR **gaiRt**-naiR)   gardener
20. **der Rechen** (daiR **Re**-Hen)   rake
21. **der Wasserschlauch** (daiR **vahs**-seR-shlowH)   garden hose
22. **die Düse** (dee **deu**-zuh)   nozzle
23. **die Terassenmöbel** (dee te-**Rah**-sen-mOE-bel)   patio furniture
24. **das Gebüsch** (dahs ge-**beush**)   bushes
25. **die Außenlichter** (dee **ow**-sen-liH-taiR)   outdoor lights
26. **der Schornstein** (daiR-**shohRn**-shtighn)   chimney
27. **das Dach** (dahs dahK)   roof
28. **die Dachschindel** (dee **dahK**-shin-del)   shingle
29. **die Dachrinne** (dee **dahK**-Rin-nuh)   gutter
30. **das Glas** (dahs glahs)   glass
31. **der Holzzaun** (daiR **hohlts**-tsown)   wooden fence

Fragen   (Questions)

1. What is "der Wasserschlauch"?
2. What tools is the woman using?
3. Name the two types of fences.
4. Who is raking the leaves?

2. Das Wohnzimmer (dahs **vohn**-tsim-maiR)   The Living Room

1. die Antenne (dee ahn-**ten**-nuh)   antenna
2. das Radio (dahs **Rah**-dee-oh)   radio
3. der Plattenspieler (daiR **plaht**-ten-shpee-laiR)   record player
4. die Schreibmaschine (dee **shRighb**-mah-shee-nuh)   typewriter
5. die Schallplatten (dee **shahl**-plaht-ten)   records
6. der Fernseher (daiR **faiRn**-zay-aiR)   television
7. das Bücherregal (dahs **bew**-HaiR-Ray-gahl)   bookcase
8. das Buch (dahs **booH**)   book
9. der Teppich (daiR **tep**-piH)   carpet
10. das Telefon (dahs **teh**-leh-fohn)   telephone
11. das Sofa (dahs **zoh**-fah)   sofa
12. die Stricknadeln (dee **shtRiK**-nah-deln)   knitting needles
13. das Garn (dahs **gahRn**)   yarn
14. der Kaffeetisch (daiR **kah**-fay-tish)   coffee table
15. der Briefumschlag (daiR **bReef**-oom-shlahg)   envelope
16. der Brief (daiR **bReef**)   letter
17. die Zeitung (dee **tsigh**-toong)   newspaper
18. die Großmutter (dee **gRohs**-muht-taiR)   grandmother
19. das Kissen (dahs **kis**-sen)   pillow
20. der Staubsauger (daiR **shtowp**-zow-gaiR)   vacuum cleaner
21. der Schaukelstuhl (daiR **show**-kel-shtool)   rocking chair
22. der Enkel (daiR **en**-kel)   grandson
23. die Katze (dee **kah**-tsuh)   cat

24. **der Holzkorb** (daiR **hohlts**-kohrp) log basket
25. **die Klötze** (dee **klOEt**-zuh) logs
26. **die Fliesen** (dee **flee**-zen) floor tiles
27. **das Feuer** (dahs **foy**-eR) fire
28. **der Kaminsims** (daiR **kah**-meen-zimz) mantel
29. **die Uhr** (dee ooR) clock
30. **das Wandbrett** (dahs **vahnt**-bRet) wall bracket
31. **der Lampenschirm** (daiR **lahmp**-pen-sheeRm) lamp shade
32. **der Spiegel** (daiR **shpee**-gel) mirror
33. **der Rahmen** (daiR **Rah**-men) frame
34. **die Gardine** (dee gahR-**dee**-nuh) curtains
35. **der Regenschirm** (daiR **Ray**-gen-sheeRm) umbrella
36. **der Schirmständer** (daiR **sheeRm**-shten-daiR) umbrella stand
37. **der Sessel** (daiR **zes**-sel) armchair
38. **die Pflanze** (dee **pflahn**-tsuh) plant
39. **das Photo** (dahs **foh**-toh) photograph

Fragen (Questions)

1. What does the grandmother have in her hands?
2. Who is playing with "die Katze"?
3. What is on the mantel?
4. What is the boy near the shelves looking for?

3. Die Küche (dee kew-Huh)   The Kitchen

1. **das Geschirrspülmittel** (dahs ge-**sheeR**-shpeul-mit-tel)   dish detergent
2. **die Spülbürste** (dee **Shpeul**-beuR-stuh)   dish brush
3. **das Kabinett** (dahs kah-bi-**net**)   kitchen cabinet
4. **das Kochbuch** (dahs **kawK**-booH)   cookbook
5. **das Spülbecken** (dahs **shpeul**-bek-ken)   sink
6. **der Wasserhahn** (daiR **vah**-saiR-hahn)   faucet
7. **der Griff** (daiR **gRif**)   handle
8. **der Hackblock** (daiR **hahk**-blohk)   chopping block
9. **die Spülmaschine** (dee **shpeul**-mah-she-nuh)   dishwasher
10. **die Schublade** (dee **shoop**-lah-duh)   drawer
11. **die Spritze** (dee **shpRits**-zuh)   sprayer
12. **das Reinigungsmittel** (dahs **Righ**-ni-goongs-mit-tel)   cleanser
13. **die Gläser** (dee **glay**-zeR)   glasses
14. **die Kuchenrolle** (dee **koo**-Ken-rol-luh)   rolling pin
15. **der Dosenschinken** (daiR **doh**-zen-shink-ken)   canned ham
16. **das Sieb** (dahs **zeep**)   sifter
17. **der Toaster** (daiR **tohs**-taiR)   toaster
18. **der Toast** (daiR **tohst**)   toast
19. **die Spachtel** (dee **shpahK**-tel)   spatula
20. **die Marmelade** (dee mahR-muh-**lah**-duh)   jam
21. **der Blender** (daiR **blent**-daiR)   blender
22. **das Meßglas** (dahs **mes**-glahs)   measuring cup
23. **die Schüssel** (dee **shews**-sel)   bowl
24. **der Handmixer** (daiR **hahnt**-miks-saiR)   hand mixer
25. **der Salzstreuer** (daiR **zahlts**-stRoy-aiR)   salt shaker
26. **der Pfefferstreuer** (daiR **pfef**-faiR-stRoy-áiR)   pepper shaker
27. **der Schöpflöffel** (daiR **shOEp**-lOEf-fel)   ladle
28. **der Kartoffelstampfer** (daiR Kahr-**tawf**-fel-shtahm-pfaiR)   potato masher
29. **die Meßlöffel** (dee **mes**-lOEf-fel)   measuring spoons
30. **die Servietten** (dee zaiR-vee-**et**-ten)   napkins
31. **die Gabel** (dee **gah**-bel)   fork
32. **das Messer** (dahs **mes**-saiR)   knife
33. **die Löffel** (dee **lOEf**-fel)   spoons
34. **die Butter** (dee **buht**-taiR)   butter

35. **der Hund** (daiR hoont)   dog
36. **das Wasser** (dahs **vahs**-saiR)   water
37. **der Kaffee** (daiR **kahf**-fay)   coffee
38. **der Deckel** (daiR **dek**-kel)   lid
39. **der Mop** (daiR mohp)   mop
40. **der Eimer** (daiR **igh**-maiR)   bucket
41. **der Lappen** (daiR **lahp**-pen)   rag
42. **der Rostbraten** (daiR **Rohst**-bRah-ten)   roast beef
43. **der Ofen** (daiR **oh**-fen)   oven
44. **die Pfanne** (dee **pfah**-nuh)   pan
45. **der Wasserkessel** (daiR **vahs**-saiR-kes-sel)   teakettle
46. **der Herd** (daiR haiRt)   range
47. **die Eier** (dee **igh**-aiR)   eggs
48. **die Bratpfanne** (dee **bRaht**-pfah-nuh)   frying pan
49. **die Mutter** (dee **moot**-teR)   mother
50. **die Kehrichtschaufel** (dee **kay**-RiHt-show-fel)   dustpan
51. **der Abfalleimer** (daiR **ahp**-fahl-igh-maiR)   trash can
52. **der Kühlschrank** (daiR **kewl**-shRahnk)   refrigerator
53. **die Taschenlampe** (dee **tah**-shen-lahm-puh)   flashlight
54. **das Tiefkühlgerät** (dahs **teef**-kewl-ge-Rayt)   freezer
55. **der Waschlappen** (daiR **vahsh**-lahp-pen)   dishcloth
56. **die Wäscheseife** (dee **vesh**-uh-zigh-fuh)   laundry detergent
57. **die Waschmaschine** (dee **vahsh**-muh-shee-nuh)   washer
58. **der Trockner** (daiR **trawk**-en-aiR)   dryer
59. **der Besen** (daiR **bay**-zen)   broom
60. **der Briefordner** (daiR **bReef**-ohRt-naiR)   letter holder
61. **der Picknickkorb** (daiR **pik**-nik-kohRp)   picnic basket
62. **der Eiskübel** (daiR **ighs**-keub-bel)   ice bucket
63. **die Tassen** (dee **tahs**-sen)   cups

Fragen   (Questions)

1. What is in "der Ofen"?
2. What is "der Hund" drinking?
3. What is in the toaster?
4. What is in the bucket?

4. Das Klassenzimmer (dahs **klahs**-sen-tsim-maiR)   The Classroom

1. **der Dinosaurier** (daiR dee-noh-**zow**-Ree-aiR)   dinosaur
2. **die Uhr** (dee ooR)   clock
3. **die Decke** (dee **dek**-kuh)   ceiling
4. **das Alphabet** (dahs **ahl**-fah-bayt)   alphabet
5. **der Schreibtisch** (daiR **shRighp**-tish)   desk
6. **die Vase** (dee **vah**-zuh)   vase
7. **der Hase** (daiR **hah**-zuh)   rabbit
8. **die Wandtafel** (dee **vahnt**-tah-fel)   blackboard
9. **die Subtraktion** (dee zoop-tRahk-tsee-**ohn**)   subtraction
10. **die Vervielfachung** (dee faiR-**feel**-faK-oong)   multiplication
11. **die Addition** (dee ah-dit-tsee-**ohn**)   addition
12. **der Schrank** (daiR shRahnk)   closet
13. **der Kalender** (daiR **kah**-len-daiR)   calendar
14. **das Photo** (dahs **foh**-toh)   photograph
15. **das Murmelspiel** (dahs **mooR**-mel-shpeel)   marbles
16. **der Globus** (daiR **gloh**-boos)   globe
17. **die Bücher** (dee **bewH**-aiR)   books
18. **die Puppen** (dee **puhp**-pen)   dolls
19. **die Schachtel** (dee **shahK**-tel)   boxes
20. **der Klebstoff** (daiR **klayp**-shtohf)   glue
21. **die Papierpuppe** (dee pah-**peeR**-poop-puh)   paper puppet
22. **die Tüte** (dee **teu**-tuh)   paper bag
23. **der Tesafilm** (daiR **tay**-zah-film)   adhesive tape
24. **die Schere** (dee **shaiR**-Ruh)   scissors
25. **der Lehm** (daiR laym)   clay
26. **der Käfig** (daiR **kay**-fig)   cage

ABCDEFGHIJKLMNOPQRSTU

$$+\ 375$$
$$149$$

$$409$$
$$\times 8$$

$$-\ 583$$
$$150$$

27. **die Buntstifte** (dee **boont**-shtif-tuh)   crayons
28. **das Lineal** (dahs li-nay-**ahl**)   ruler
29. **der Pinsel** (daiR **pin**-zel)   paintbrush
30. **die Kreide** (dee **kRigh**-duH)   chalk
31. **die Farbe** (dee **fahRb**-buh)   paint
32. **die Reißzwecke** (dee **Righs**-tsvek-kuh)   tacks
33. **die Bauklötze** (dee **bow**-klOEts-suh)   building blocks
34. **die Staffelei** (dee shtah-fel-**igh**)   easel
35. **die Wasserfarben** (dee **vahs**-saiR-fahR-ben)   watercolor
36. **der Arbeitskittel** (daiR **ahR**-bights-kit-tel)   smock
37. **der Schwamm** (daiR **shvahm**)   eraser
38. **das Papier** (dahs pah-**peeR**)   paper
39. **die Bleistifte** (dee **bligh**-shtif-tuh)   pencils
40. **der Student** (daiR shtew-**dent**)   student
41. **der Papierkorb** (daiR pah-**peeR**-kohRp)   wastebasket
42. **die Zeichnungen** (dee **tsighH**-noong-gen)   drawings
43. **das Aquarium** (dahs ah-**qvah**-Ree-oom)   aquarium
44. **der Fish** (daiR fish)   fish
45. **das Fenster** (dahs **fen**-staiR)   window
46. **das Schwein** (dahs **shvighn**)   pig
47. **der Vogel** (daiR **foh**-gel)   bird
48. **die Katze** (dee **kaht**-tsuh)   cat
49. **der Affe** (daiR **ahf**-fuh)   monkey
50. **die Karte** (dee **kahR**-tuh)   map
51. **der Spitzer** (daiR **shpit**-saiR)   pencil sharpener
52. **der Bleistifthalter** (daiR **bligh**-shtift-hal-taiR)   pencil holder
53. **das Heft** (dahs heft)   notebook
54. **die Lehrerin** (dee **laiR**-RaiR-Rin)   teacher

Fragen   (Questions)

1. What do you use to cut paper?
2. Name the three math problems on the blackboard.
3. What is the girl at the easel wearing?
4. Name the objects hanging on the left wall.

5. Die Kleidung (dee **kligh**-toong)   Clothing

1. **der Hut** (daiR hoot)   hat
2. **die Brille** (dee **bRil**-luh)   glasses
3. **das Kleid** (dahs klight)   dress
4. **der Badeanzug** (daiR **bah**-duh-ahn-tsoog)   bathing suit
5. **die Handtasche** (dee **hahnt**-tah-shuh)   purse
6. **die Schneestiefel** (dee **shnay**-stee-fel)   snow boots
7. **die Hausschuhe** (dee **hows**-shoo-huh)   slippers
8. **die Schuhe mit hohen Absätzen** (dee **shoo**-uh mit **hoh**-hen **ahp**-zets-zen)
   high-heeled shoes
9. **der Pullover** (daiR pool-**oh**-faiR)   sweater
10. **der Rock** (daiR Rohck)   skirt
11. **die Schuhe** (dee **shoo**-uh)   shoes
12. **die Sandalen** (dee zahn-**dah**-len)   sandals

13. **die Jacke** (dee **yah**-kuh)   jacket
14. **die Mütze** (dee **moo**-tsuh)   cap
15. **der Mantel** (daiR **mahn**-tel)   coat
16. **die Krawatte** (dee kRah-**vah**-tuh)   tie
17. **die Fliege** (dee **fleeg**-guh)   bow tie
18. **der Regenmantel** (daiR **Ray**-gen-mahn-tel)   raincoat
19. **das Langärmelhemd** (dahs **lahng**-aiR-mel-hemt)   long-sleeved shirt
20. **die Weste** (dee **ves**-tuh)   vest
21. **der Gürtel** (daiR **geuR**-tel)   belt
22. **der Bademantel** (daiR **bah**-duh-mahn-tel)   bathrobe
23. **die Hosen** (dee **hoh**-zen)   pants
24. **die Unterwäsche** (dee **oon**-taiR-vesh-uh)   underwear
25. **die Socken** (dee **zaw**-ken)   socks
26. **der Pyjama** (daiR pee-**yah**-ma)   pajamas
27. **die Tennisschuhe** (dee **ten**-nis-shoo-uh)   tennis shoes

Fragen   (Questions)

1. What might you wear to help you see better?
2. What do you wear to bed?
3. What do you wear inside your shoes?
4. What do you wear to go swimming?

6. Die Jahreszeiten und das Wetter

(dee **yahR**-Res-tsigh-ten oont dahs **vet**-teR)

The Seasons and the Weather

1. **der Sommer** (daiR **zoh**-maiR)   summer
2. **der Frühling** (daiR **fReu**-ling)   spring
3. **der Winter** (daiR **vin**-taiR)   winter
4. **der Herbst** (daiR haiRbst)   fall

5. **die Sonne** (dee **zohn**-nuh)   sun
6. **die Wolken** (dee **vohl**-ken)   clouds
7. **der Mond** (daiR mohnt)   moon
8. **der Regenbogen** (daiR **Ray**-gen-boh-gen)   rainbow
9. **warm** (vahRm)   hot
10. **der Blitz** (daiR blitz)   lightning
11. **der Regen** (daiR **Ray**-gen)   rain
12. **kalt** (kahlt)   cold
13. **der Schnee** (daiR shnay)   snow

Fragen   (Questions)

1. What do you see after it rains?
2. What is the warmest season of the year?
3. What do you see during a thunderstorm?
4. What do you see in the sky at night?

7. Der Sport (daiR spɔhRt) Sports

1. **das Fechten** (dahs **feH**-ten) fencing
2. **das Tennis** (dahs **ten**-nis) tennis
3. **das Ringen** (dahs **Ring**-gen) wrestling
4. **das Radfahren** (dahs **Raht**-fah-Ren) cycling
5. **das Skifahren** (dahs **skee**-fah-Ren) skiing
6. **das Kegeln** (dahs **kay**-geln) bowling
7. **das Korbballspiel** (dahs **kohRp**-bahl-shpeel) basketball

8. **das Boxen** (dahs **bohks**-sen) boxing
9. **das Baseball** (dahs **bays**-bahl) baseball
10. **das Judo** (dahs **yoo**-doh) judo
11. **das Wasserskilaufen** (dahs **vahs**-saiR-skee-lowf-fen) waterskiing
12. **das amerikanische Fußballspiel**
    (dahs ah-may-ri-**kahn**-ni-shuh **foos**-bahl-shpeel) football

Fragen (Questions)

1. For which sport do you need a bat?
2. For which sports do you need skis?
3. Name a sport for which you need a bicycle.
4. What sport do you play in a bowling alley?

8. Die Stadt (dee shtaht)   The City

1. das Gebäude (dahs ge-**boy**-duh)   building
2. das Blumengeschäft (dahs **bloo**-men-ge-sheft)   flower shop
3. der Spielwarenladen (daiR **shpeel**-vah-Ren-lah-den)   toy store
4. die Bushaltestelle (dee **boos**-hahlt-tuh-shtel-luh)   bus stop
5. die Bank (dee bahnk)   bench
6. die Bäckerei (dee beck-aiR-**igh**)   bakery
7. die Plane (dee **plah**-nuh)   awning
8. die Fußgängerin (dee **foos**-geng-aiR-Rin)   pedestrian
9. der Schulbus (daiR **shool**-boos)   school bus
10. der Fahrer (daiR **fahR**-RaiR)   driver
11. der Kombiwagen (daiR **kohm**-bee-vah-gen)   van
12. die Verkehrsampel (dee **faiR**-kaiRs-ahm-pel)   traffic light
13. das Taxi (dahs **tah**-ksee)   taxi
14. die Straße (dee **shtRah**-suh)   street
15. der Lastkraftwagen (daiR **lahst**-kRahft-vah-gen)   truck
16. die Tankstelle (dee **tahnk**-shtel-luh)   gas station
17. die Benzinpumpe (dee ben-**tseen**-poom-puh)   gas pump

18. **die Fußgängerkreuzung** (dee **foos**-geng-aiR-kRoy-tsoong)   pedestrian crossing
19. **der Erdbagger** (daiR **aiRt**-bahg-gaiR)   bulldozer
20. **das Rohr** (dahs RohR)   pipe
21. **das Loch** (dahs lohK)   hole
22. **der Briefkasten** (daiR **bReef**-kahs-sten)   mailbox
23. **die Straßenlaterne** (dee **shtRah**-sen-lah-taiR-nuh)   street light
24. **der Feuerwehrmann** (daiR **foy**-aiR-vaiR-mahn)   fireman
25. **das Beil** (dahs bighl)   ax
26. **die Leiter** (dee **ligh**-taiR)   ladder
27. **das Feuerwehrauto** (dahs **foy**-aiR-vaiR-ow-toh)   fire truck
28. **der Polizist** (daiR poh-li-**tsist**)   policeman
29. **der Unfall** (daiR **oon**-fahl)   accident
30. **die Sirene** (dee zee-**Ray**-nuh)   siren
31. **der Polizeiwagen** (daiR poh-li-**tsigh**-vah-gen)   police car
32. **der Hydrant** (daiR-hoo-**dRahnt**)   fire hydrant
33. **der Baum** (daiR bowm)   tree
34. **der Rettungswagen** (daiR **Ret**-toongs-vah-gen)   ambulance
35. **der Abschleppwagen** (daiR **ahp**-shlepp-vah-gen)   tow truck
36. **die Parkuhr** (dee **pahRk**-oohR)   parking meter
37. **der Spielplatz** (daiR **shpeel**-plahts)   playground

Fragen   (Questions)

1. What happened to the two cars in the intersection?
2. If you are hurt, you are taken to the hospital in _____?
3. Who is directing the traffic?
4. What is "die Verkehrsampel"?

9. Der Supermarkt (daiR zoo-paiR-mahRkt)   The Supermarket

1. **das Eis** (dahs ighs)   ice cream
2. **die Flasche** (dee **flah**-shuh)   bottle
3. **der Zucker** (daiR **tsoo**-kaiR)   sugar
4. **die Erdnußbutter** (dee **aiRd**-noos-boot-taiR)   peanut butter
5. **das Schokoladeneis** (dahs shawk-oh-**lah**-den-ighs)   chocolate ice cream
6. **die Dose** (dee **doh**-zuh)   can
7. **der Einkaufswagen** (daiR **ighn**-kowfs-vah-gen)   shopping cart
8. **die Marmelade** (dee mahR-muh-**lah**-duh)   jam
9. **das Brot** (dahs bRoht)   bread
10. **die Waage** (dee **vah**-guh)   scale
11. **die Kirschen** (dee **keeR**-shen)   cherries
12. **die Himbeeren** (dee **him**-baiR-Ren)   raspberries
13. **die Trauben** (dee **tRow**-ben)   grapes
14. **die Bananen** (dee bah-**nah**-nen)   bananas
15. **die Papayas** (dee pah-**pigh**-yahs)   papayas
16. **die Erdbeeren** (dee **aiRt**-baiR-Ren)   strawberries
17. **das Obst** (dahs ohpst)   fruit
18. **der Verkäufer** (daiR **faiR**-koy-faiR)   grocer
19. **die Lebensmittel** (dee **lay**-benz-mit-tel)   groceries
20. **die Tüte** (dee **teu**-tuh)   paper bag
21. **die Kassiererin** (dee kahs-**see**-RaiR-Rin)   cashier
22. **die Kasse** (dee **kahs**-suh)   cash register
23. **die Quittung** (dee **kvi**-toong)   receipt
24. **der Einkaufskorb** (daiR **ighn**-kowfs-kohrp)   grocery basket

Fragen   (Questions)

1. What is the girl getting from the freezer?
2. Name all the vegetables that start with the letter "k."
3. Who is behind the cash register?
4. Who is packing the groceries?

25. die Kartoffel (dee kahR-**taw**-fel)   potatoes
26. die Karotten (dee kah-**Raw**-ten)   carrots
27. die Zwiebeln (dee **tsvee**-beln)   onions
28. die Bohnen (dee **boh**-nen)   beans
29. die Tomaten (dee toh-**mah**-ten)   tomatoes
30. die Kohle (dee **koh**-luh)   cabbages
31. die Auberginen (dee oh-baiR-**zhee**-nen)   eggplants
32. der Salat (daiR zah-**laht**)   lettuce
33. der Mais (daiR mighs)   corn
34. die Birnen (dee **beeR**-nen)   pears
35. der Kürbis (daiR **keuR**-bees)   squash
36. der Spargel (daiR **shpahR**-gel)   asparagus
37. die Paprikaschoten (dee pap-**Ree**-kah-sho-ten)   bell peppers
38. der Blumenkohl (daiR **bloo**-men-kohl)   cauliflower
39. die Pflaumen (dee **pflow**-men)   plums
40. die Zitronen (dee tsi-**tRoh**-nen)   lemons
41. die Pfirsiche (dee **pfeeR**-zi-shuh)   peaches
42. die Äpfel (dee **ep**-fel)   apples
43. der Kuchen (daiR **koo**-Hen)   cake
44. die Obsttorte (dee **ohbst**-tohR-tuh)   pie
45. die Törtchen (dee **tOERt**-Hen)   cupcake
46. der Thunfisch (daiR **toon**-fish)   tuna
47. der Saft (daiR zahft)   juice
48. die Handcreme (dee **hahnt**-kray-muh)   hand cream
49. das Mehl (dahs mayl)   flour
50. die Cornflakes (dee **korn**-flayks)   cereal
51. das Regal (dahs Ray-**gahl**)   shelf
52. der Arbeiter (daiR **ahR**-bigh-taiR)   worker
53. die Kekse (dee **kek**-suh)   cookies
54. die Milch (dee milH)   milk
55. der Käse (daiR **kay**-zuh)   cheese
56. die Würste (dee **veuR**-stuh)   sausages
57. die Eier (dee **igh**-aiR)   eggs
58. das Hammelfleisch (dahs **hah**-mal-flighsh)   lamb
59. die Butter (dee **boo**-taiR)   butter
60. die Hühnchen (dee **hoon**-Hen)   chickens
61. die Krabben (dee **kRahp**-pen)   crabs
62. die Fische (dee **fish**-uh)   fish

10. Im Restaurant (im Res-tau-**Rahnt**)   In the Restaurant

1. **die Pflanze** (dee **pflahn**-tsuh)   plant
2. **der Blumentopf** (daiR **bloo**-men-tawpf)   flowerpot
3. **der Kamin** (daiR **kah**-meen)   fireplace
4. **der Tisch** (daiR tish)   table
5. **der Stuhl** (daiR shtool)   chair
6. **das Glas** (dahs glahs)   glass
7. **der Teller** (daiR **tel**-laiR)   plate
8. **die Tischdecke** (dee **tish**-deck-kuh)   tablecloth
9. **der Salat** (daiR zah-**laht**)   salad
10. **die Zange** (dee **tsahn**-guh)   tongs
11. **das Eis** (dahs ighs)   ice
12. **das Steak** (dahs shtayk)   steak
13. **der Kuchen** (daiR **koo**-Hen)   cake
14. **der Speck** (daiR shpek)   bacon
15. **die Spiegeleier** (dee **shpee**-gel-igh-aiR)   fried eggs
16. **die Teekanne** (dee **tay**-kah-nuh)   teapot
17. **der Hühnerbraten** (daiR **heuh**-naiR-bRah-ten)   roast chicken
18. **der Krug** (daiR kRoog)   pitcher
19. **die Rechnung** (dee **ReH**-noong)   check
20. **die Marmelade** (dee mahR-meh-**lah**-duh)   jam
21. **die Speisekarte** (dee **shpigh**-zuh-kahR-tuh)   menu
22. **das Salz** (dahs zahlts)   salt
23. **der Pfeffer** (daiR **pfef**-faiR)   pepper
24. **die Untertasse** (dee **oont**-taiR-tahs-suh)   saucer
25. **die Tasse** (dee **tahs**-suh)   cup
26. **die Serviette** (dee zaiR-vee-**et**-tuh)   napkin
27. **das belegte Brot** (dahs be-layg-te **bRoht**)   sandwich
28. **der Hamburger** (daiR **hahm**-booR-gaiR)   hamburger

29. **die Würste** (dee **veuR**-stuh)   sausages
30. **die Salami** (dee zah-**lah**-mee)   salami
31. **der Küchenchef** (daiR **keu**-Hen-shef)   chef
32. **die Kellnerin** (dee **kel**-naiR-Rin)   waitress
33. **die Schürze** (dee **sheuRts-suh)**   apron
34. **die Metallschüssel** (dee meh-**tahl**-sheus-sel)   metal bowl
35. **der Schinken** (daiR **shink**-ken)   ham
36. **die gefüllten Eier** (dee ge-**feul**-ten **igh**-aiR)   stuffed eggs
37. **der Kelch** (daiR kelH)   goblet
38. **der Tee** (daiR tay)   tea
39. **die Schneidemaschine** (dee **shnigh**-duh-mah-shee-nuh)   meat slicer
40. **das Spülbecken** (dahs **shpeul**-bek-ken)   sink
41. **das schmutzige Geschirr** (dahs **shmoots**-tsig-guh ge-**sheeR)**   dirty dishes
42. **die Kaffeekanne** (dee **kah**-fay-kah-nuh)   coffeepot

Fragen   (Questions)

1. Who is cooking in the kitchen?
2. Who is bringing the salad bowl?
3. What is the boy eating?
4. What does the girl have in her hands?

11. Das Postamt (dahs **pohst**-ahmt)   The Post Office

1. **die Fahne** (dee **fah**-nuh)   flag
2. **das Postamt** (dahs **pohst**-ahmt)   post office
3. **die Ladestelle** (dee **lah**-duh-shtel-luh)   loading dock
4. **der Eingang** (daiR **ighn**-gahng)   entrance
5. **der Postwagen** (daiR **pohst**-vah-gen)   mail truck
6. **der Briefkasten** (daiR **bReef**-kah-sten)   mailbox
7. **der Briefträger** (daiR **bReef**-tRay-gaiR)   letter carrier
8. **der Briefsack** (daiR **bReef**-zahk)   mail bag
9. **der Preis** (daiR **pRighs**)   price
10. **die Waage** (dee **vah**-guh)   scale
11. **das Paket** (dahs pah-**kayt**)   package
12. **die Briefmarke** (dee **bReef**-mahR-kuh)   stamp
13. **der Brief** (daiR **bReef**)   letter
14. **die Adresse** (dee ah-**dRes**-suh)   address
15. **der Postbeamte** (daiR **pohst**-be-ahmt-tuh)   postal worker
16. **der Pack Briefe** (daiR pahk **bReef**-fuh)   bundled letters
17. **die Zeitung** (dee **tsigh**-toong)   newspaper
18. **die Zeitschriften** (dee **tsight**-shRift-en)   magazines

Fragen   (Questions)

1. Where do you go to mail letters?
2. What must you put on an envelope?
3. Who delivers the mail?
4. What is "die Zeitung"?

12. Die Bank (dee bahnk)   The Bank

1. **der Aktenschrank** (daiR **ahk**-ten-shRahnk)   file cabinet
2. **das Gemälde** (dahs ge-**meld**-duh)   painting
3. **die Wache** (dee **vaK**-huh)   guard
4. **der Tresor** (daiR tray-**zohR**)   safe
5. **das Bankfach** (dahs **bahnk**-faK)   safe deposit box
6. **die Kundin** (dee **koond**-din)   client
7. **das Scheckbuch** (dahs **shek**-booK)   checkbook
8. **die Kreditkarte** (dee kRe-**deet**-kahR-tuh)   credit card
9. **die Scheine** (dee **shigh**-nuh)   bills
10. **die Münze** (dee **meun**-tsuh)   coins
11. **das Einzahlungsformular** (dahs **ighn**-tsahl-loongs-foR-muh-lahR)   deposit slip
12. **der Kugelschreiber** (daiR **koo**-gel-shRigh-baiR)   pen
13. **der Scheck** (daiR shek)   check
14. **der Geldbeutel** (daiR **gelt**-boyt-tel)   money bag
15. **der Kassierer** (daiR kahs-**see**-ReR)   bank teller

Fragen   (Questions)

1. Name a place where you keep valuables.
2. Name a room where money is locked in.
3. Who is standing near the vault?
4. What do you need to make a deposit?

13. Beim Arzt (bighm ahRtst)   At the Doctor's Office

1. **der Blutdruck** (daiR **bloot**-dRook)   blood pressure
2. **die Krankenschwester** (dee **krahn**-ken-shves-taiR)   nurse
3. **die Armbanduhr** (dee **ahRm**-bahnt-oohR)   watch
4. **das Thermometer** (dahs taiR-moh-**may**-taiR)   thermometer
5. **die Nadel** (dee **nah**-del)   needle
6. **die Spritze** (dee **shpRit**-suh)   syringe
7. **die Pillen** (dee **pil**-len)   pills
8. **die Technikerin** (dee tek-ni-**kaiR**-Rin)   technician
9. **der Handschuh** (daiR **hahnt**-shoo)   glove
10. **der Gipsverband** (daiR **gips**-faiR-bahnt)   cast
11. **die Augentafel** (dee **ow**-gen-tah-fel)   eye chart
12. **der Hörtest** (daiR **hOER**-test)   hearing test
13. **der Ohrenspiegel** (daiR **ohR**-en-shpee-gel)   otoscope
14. **das Baby** (dahs **bay**-bee)   baby
15. **das Stethoskop** (dahs **shtay**-toh-skohp)   stethoscope
16. **der Kinderarzt** (daiR **kin**-daiR-ahRtst)   pediatrician
17. **das Rezept** (dahs Ray-**tsept**)   prescription

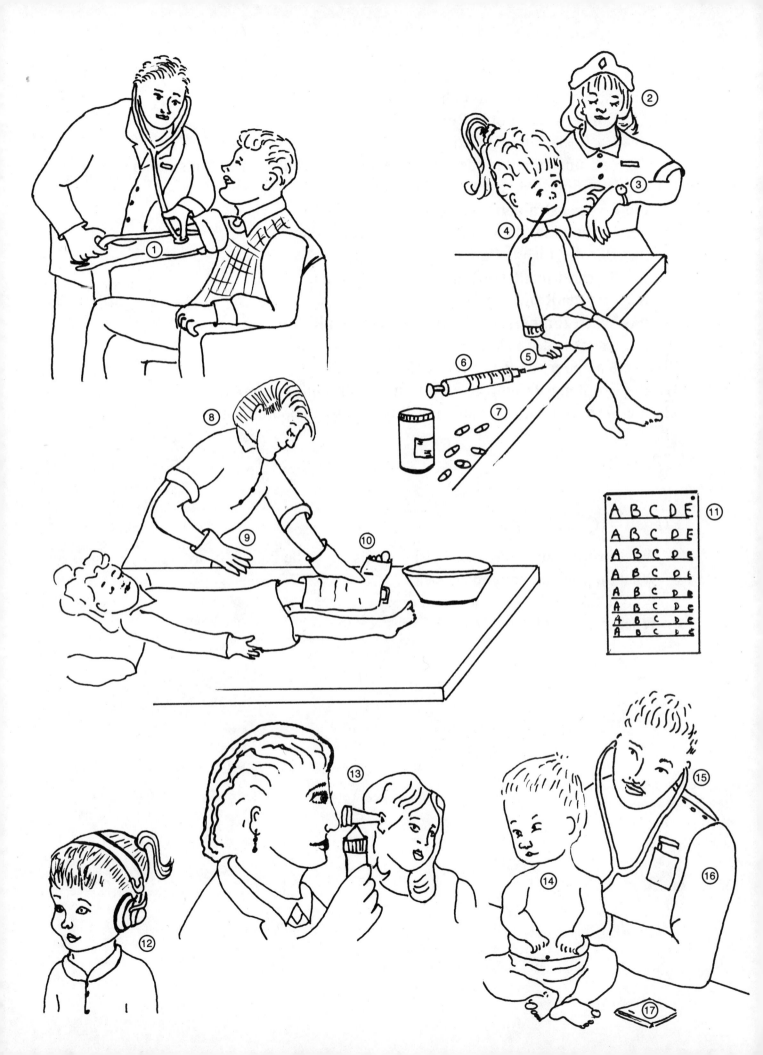

18. **die Plombe** (dee **plohm**-buh)   filling
19. **der Bohrer** (daiR **bohR**-ReR)   drill
20. **das Loch** (dahs lohK)   cavity
21. **die Zahninstrumente** (dee **tsahn**-in-stroo-men-tuh)   dental instruments
22. **die Klammer** (dee **klahm**-maiR)   braces
23. **die Röntgenstrahlen** (dee **ROEnt**-gen-shtrahl-len)   X ray
24. **der Orthopäde** (daiR ohR-toh-**pay**-duh)   orthopedist
25. **das Pflaster** (dahs **pflahs**-staiR)   bandage
26. **der Tierarzt** (daiR **teeR**-ahRtst)   veterinarian
27. **der Lift** (daiR lift)   elevator
28. **das Wartezimmer** (dahs **vahR**-tuh-tsim-maiR)   waiting room
29. **die Krücke** (dee **kReuk**-kuh)   crutch
30. **der Kalender** (daiR kah-**len**-daiR)   calendar
31. **die Empfangsdame** (dee emp-**fahngs**-dah-muh)   receptionist
32. **die Verabredung** (dee faiR-**ahp**-Ray-doong)   appointment

Fragen   (Questions)

1. What instrument is the doctor using to listen to the baby's heart?
2. What do you call an animal doctor?
3. Who is taking the girl's temperature?
4. What is "das Pflaster"?

JUNI

14. Die Tankstelle (dee **tahnk**-shtel-luh)   The Service Station

1. **das Hebewerk** (dahs **hay**-buh-vaiRk)   hydraulic lift
2. **der zerspaltene Windschutzschirm**
   (daiR tsaiR-**shpahl**-ten-nuh **vint**-shoots-sheeRm)   cracked windshield
3. **die Autowaschanlage** (dee **ow**-toh-vah-shahn-lah-guh)   car wash
4. **die gekerbte Tür** (dee ge-**kaiRbt**-tuh teuR)   dented door
5. **der Abschleppwagen** (daiR **ahp**-shlep-vah-gen)   tow truck
6. **die Benzinpumpe** (dee ben-**tseen**-poom-puh)   gas pump
7. **der Tankwart** (daiR **tahnk**-wahrt)   attendant
8. **der Kanister** (daiR **kah**-nis-taiR)   can
9. **der Tankdeckel** (daiR **tahnk**-dek-kel)   gas cap
10. **der Kofferraum** (daiR **kohf**-faiR-Rowm)   trunk
11. **das Dach** (dahs dahK)   roof
12. **der Sits** (daiR zits)   seat
13. **die Tür** (dee teuR)   door
14. **der Reifen** (daiR **Righ**-fen)   tire
15. **das Nummernschild** (dahs **noom**-maiRn-shilt)   license plate
16. **die Stoßstange** (dee **shtohs**-shtahng-guh)   bumper
17. **der Scheinwerfer** (daiR **shighn**-vaiR-faiR)   headlight
18. **die Schutzhaube** (dee **shoots**-howb-buh)   hood
19. **die Scheibenwischer** (dee **shighb**-ben-vish-aiR)   windshield wipers
20. **das Lenkrad** (dahs **lenk**-Raht)   steering wheel

21. **die Ölkanne** (dee **OEl**-kahn-nuh)   oil can
22. **der Kühler** (daiR **keuhl**-laiR)   radiator
23. **der Werkzeugkasten** (daiR **vaiRk**-tsoyg-kahs-ten)   toolbox
24. **die Batterie** (dee bah-taiR-Ree)   battery
25. **das Startkabel** (dahs **shtahrt**-kah-bel)   jumper cables
26. **der Schraubenzieher** (daiR **shRowb**-ben-tsee-haiR)   screwdriver
27. **der Hammer** (daiR **hah**-maiR)   hammer
28. **der Schraubschüssel** (daiR **shRowb**-sheus-sel)   wrench
29. **die Schraubenmutter** (dee **shRowb**-ben-moot-taiR)   nut
30. **die Schraube** (dee **shRowb**-buh)   screw
31. **das Rad** (dahs Raht)   wheel
32. **der Feuerlöscher** (daiR **foy**-aiR-lOE-shaiR)   fire extinguisher
33. **die Reifen** (dee **Righ**-fen)   tires
34. **die Luftpumpe** (dee **looft**-poomp-puh)   air pump
35. **der platte Reifen** (daiR **plaht**-tuh **righ**-fen)   flat tire
36. **der Mechaniker** (daiR meh-**kahn**-i-kaiR)   mechanic

Fragen   (Questions)

1. What do you call a person who repairs cars?
2. What is "die Benzinpumpe"?
3. What kind of a truck do you see in this picture?
4. Name a place where you take the car to have it washed.

15. Die Verkehrsmittel (dee **faiR**-kaiRs-mit-tel)   Transportation

1. **die Einschienbahn** (dee **ighn**-sheen-bahn)   monorail
2. **der Zug** (daiR tsoog)   train
3. **die Kabelbahn** (dee **kah**-bel-bahn)   cable car
4. **das Auto** (dahs **ow**-toh)   automobile
5. **der Lastkraftwagen** (daiR **lahst**-kRahft-vah-gen)   truck
6. **der Bus** (daiR boos)   bus
7. **das Motorrad** (dahs moh-**tohR**-Raht)   motorcycle
8. **das Fahrrad** (dahs **fahR**-Raht)   bicycle

9. **das Flugzeug** (dahs **floog**-tsoyg)   airplane
10. **der Heißluftballoon** (daiR **highs**-looft-bahl-lohn)   hot-air balloon
11. **die Rakete** (dee Rah-**kay**-tuh)   rocket
12. **der Fallschirm** (daiR **fahl**-sheeRm)   parachute
13. **der Hubschrauber** (daiR **hoop**-shRow-baiR)   helicopter
14. **das Schiff** (dahs shif)   ship
15. **das Boot** (dahs boht)   boat
16. **das Unterseeboot** (dahs **oon**-taiR-zay-boht)   submarine
17. **der Lastkahn** (daiR **lahst**-kahn)   barge
18. **das Kanu** (dahs **kah**-noo)   canoe

Fragen   (Questions)

1. What would you have with you if you jumped out of an airplane?
2. Name two vehicles that have two wheels.
3. Name a vehicle that travels under water.
4. What vehicle in this picture can go to the moon?

16. Der Bauernhof (daiR bow-aiRn-hohf)   The Farm

1. **das Feld** (dahs felt)   field
2. **die Windmühle** (dee **vint**-meuh-luh)   windmill
3. **der Hügel** (daiR **heu**-gel)   hill
4. **das Tal** (dahs tahl)   valley
5. **der Wasserfall** (daiR **vahs**-saiR-fahl)   waterfall
6. **die Kirche** (dee **keeR**-Huh)   church
7. **der Turm** (daiR tooRm)   steeple
8. **das Häuschen** (dahs **hoyz**-Hen)   cottage
9. **das Wasserrad** (dahs **vahs**-saiR-Raht)   waterwheel
10. **das Korral** (dahs koR-**Rahl**)   corral
11. **der Stall** (daiR shtahl)   stable
12. **das Faß** (dahs fahs)   barrel
13. **der Bulle** (daiR **buhl**-luh)   bull
14. **das Lasso** (dahs **lahz**-zoh)   lasso
15. **der Cowboy** (daiR **cow**-boy)   cowboy
16. **das Pferd** (dahs pfaiRt)   horse
17. **der Cowboyhut** (daiR **cow**-boy-hoot)   cowboy hat
18. **der Sattel** (daiR **zaht**-tel)   saddle
19. **die Kuh** (dee koo)   cow
20. **die Bäuerin** (dee **boy**-aiR-Rin)   farmer
21. **der Hocker** (daiR **hohk**-kaiR)   stool
22. **das Melken** (dahs **melk**-ken)   milking
23. **die Hacke** (dee **hahk**-kuh)   hoe
24. **der Rechen** (daiR **Re**-Hen)   rake
25. **die Heugabel** (dee **hoy**-gahb-bel)   pitchfork
26. **der Schaufel** (daiR **show**-fel)   shovel
27. **das Schaf** (dahs shahf)   sheep
28. **der Truthahn** (daiR **tRoot**-hahn)   turkey
29. **die Gans** (dee gahnz)   goose
30. **die Scheune** (dee **shoyn**-nuh)   barn
31. **das Heu** (dahs hoy)   hay

32. **das bewässerte Feld** (dahs be-**ves**-saiR-tuh felt)   irrigated field
33. **die Vogelscheuche** (dee **foh**-gel-shoy-Huh)   scarecrow
34. **der Traktor** (daiR **tRahk**-tohR)   tractor
35. **der Landarbeiter** (daiR **lahnt**-ahR-bight-taiR)   field hand
36. **das Silo** (dahs **zigh**-loh)   silo
37. **der Heuboden** (daiR **hoy**-boh-den)   loft
38. **der Matsch** (daiR mahtsh)   mud
39. **das Schwein** (dahs shvighn)   hog
40. **der Schweinestall** (daiR **shvighn**-nuh-shtahl)   pigpen
41. **der Hühnerstall** (daiR **heuh**-naiR-shtahl)   henhouse
42. **das Huhn** (dahs hoon)   hen
43. **die Schranke** (dee **shRahnk**-kuh)   gate
44. **der Schubkarren** (daiR **shoop**-kahR-Ren)   wheelbarrow
45. **der Obstspritzer** (daiR **ohpst**-shpRits-saiR)   fruit sprayer
46. **der Sack Weizen** (daiR zahk **vigh**-tsen)   bag of wheat
47. **die Ziege** (dee **tseeg**-guh)   goat
48. **das Gras** (dahs gRahs)   grass
49. **der Brunnen** (daiR **bRoon**-nen)   well
50. **das Bauernhaus** (dahs **bow**-aiRn-hows)   farmhouse

Fragen   (Questions)

1. Who is milking the cow?
2. Horses are kept in _____.
3. Name all the animals on the farm.
4. What do you call the place where the hogs are kept?

17. Die Tiere im Zoo (dee **teeR**-Ruh im tsoh)   Animals in the Zoo

1. **die Giraffe** (dee geeR-**ahf**-fuh)   giraffe
2. **der Elefant** (daiR **e**-le-fahnt)   elephant
3. **das Zebra** (dahs **tsay**-bRah)   zebra
4. **das Murmeltier** (dahs **mooR**-mel-teeR)   marmot
5. **das Reh** (dahs Ray)   deer
6. **der Löwe** (daiR **loe**-vuh)   lion
7. **der Leopard** (daiR lay-oh-**pahRt**)   leopard

8. **der Papagei** (daiR pah-pah-**gigh**) parrot
9. **der Quetzal** (daiR **kvet**-tsahl) quetzal
10. **das Nashorn** (dahs **nahs**-hohRn) rhinoceros
11. **der Koala** (daiR koh-**ahl**-lah) koala bear
12. **die Schlange** (dee **shlahng**-guh) snake
13. **der Schimpanse** (daiR shim-pahn-**zay**) chimpanzee
14. **der Eisbär** (daiR **ighs**-bayR) polar bear

Fragen   (Questions)

1. Name an animal with a very long neck.
2. Which animal lives in the Arctic?
3. Name two birds in the picture.
4. Which animal has antlers?

18. Am Strand (ahm shtRahnt)   At the Beach

1. die Wohnhäuser (dee **vohn**-hoy-zaiR)   apartments
2. der Leuchtturm (daiR **loyHt**-tooRm)   lighthouse
3. die Insel (dee **in**-zel)   island
4. das Schnellboot (dahs **shnel**-boht)   speedboat
5. der Kai (daiR **kigh**)   pier
6. der Bademeister (daiR **bah**-duh-migh-staiR)   lifeguard
7. der Kokosnußbaum (daiR **koh**-kohz-noos-bowm)   coconut tree
8. das Ufer (dahs **oo**-faiR)   seashore
9. der Schwimmer (daiR **shvim**-maiR)   swimmer
10. das Surfbrett (dahs **zooRf**-bRet)   surfboard
11. das Reiten (dahs **Right**-ten)   horseback riding
12. die Kamera (dee **kah**-mai-Rah)   camera
13. das Treibholz (dahs **tRighp**-hohlts)   driftwood
14. das Radio (dahs **Rah**-dee-oh)   radio
15. der Sand (daiR **zahnt**)   sand
16. der Klappstuhl (daiR **klahp**-shtool)   folding chair
17. der Sonnenschirm (daiR **zohn**-nen-sheeRm)   parasol
18. das Picknick (dahs **pik**-nik)   picnic
19. die Thermosflasche (dee **taiR**-mohs-flah-shuh)   thermos
20. das Sonnenöl (dahs **zohn**-nen-OEl)   suntan lotion
21. der Strandball (daiR **shtRahnt**-bahl)   beach ball
22. die Fußstapfe (dee **foos**-shtahpf-fuh)   footprint

23. **die Muschelschale** (dee **moos**-shel-shahl-luh) seashell
24. **der Seetang** (daiR **zay**-tahng) seaweed
25. **die Muschel** (dee **moo**-shel) clam
26. **die Sandburg** (dee **zahnd**-booRg) sand castle
27. **die Flossen** (dee **flo**-sen) fins
28. **der Rettungsring** (daiR **Ret**-toongs-Ring) lifesaver
29. **die Taucherbrille** (dee **tow**-HeR-bRil-luh) goggles
30. **die Palme** (dee **pahlm**-muh) palm tree
31. **das Badetuch** (dahs **bah**-duh-tooH) beach towel
32. **das Ruder** (dahs **Roo**-daiR) oar
33. **das Ruderboot** (dahs **Roo**-daiR-boht) rowboat
34. **die Seemöwe** (dee **zay**-mOE-vuh) sea gull
35. **die Robbe** (dee **Rohp**-puh) seal
36. **das Schlauchboot** (dahs **shlowK**-boht) inflatable boat
37. **der Seelöwe** (daiR **zay**-lOEv-vuh) sea lion
38. **die Welle** (dee **vel**-luh) wave
39. **der Hut** (daiR hoot) hat
40. **das Segelboot** (dahs **zay**-gel-boht) sailboat
41. **das Wasserskifahren** (dahs **vahs**-saiR-skee-fah-Ren) waterskiing
42. **der Ozeandampfer** (daiR **o**-tsay-ahn-dahm-pfaiR) ocean liner

Fragen (Questions)

1. What do you call an umbrella that protects you from the sun?
2. What are the children building?
3. Name the animals on the beach.
4. Where is "der Leuchtturm" located?

19. Der Zirkus (daiR tseeR-koos) The Circus

1. der Kopfstand (daiR kohpf-shtahnt) headstand
2. die Akrobaten (dee ahk-kroh-baht-ten) acrobats
3. der Tiger (daiR tee-gaiR) tiger
4. das Feuer (dahs foy-aiR) fire
5. der Feuerring (daiR foy-aiR-Ring) ring of fire
6. die Peitsche (dee pight-shuh) whip
7. der Trainer (daiR tRayn-aiR) trainer
8. der Löwe (daiR lOEv-vuh) lion
9. die Sicherheitskette (dee ziH-aiR-hights-ket-tuh) safety cord
10. der Sicherheitsgurt (daiR ziH-aiR-hights-gooRt) safety belt
11. der Sattellosereiter (daiR zaht-tel-loh-zuh-Right-taiR) bareback rider
12. die Federn (dee fay-daiRn) feathers
13. das Kostüm (dahs kohs-teum) costume
14. die Zuckerwatte (dee tsook-aiR-vah-tuh) cotton candy
15. der Clown (daiR klown) clown

16. **die Zuschauer** (dee **tsoo**-show-aiR)   audience
17. **die Parade** (dee pah-**Rah**-duh)   parade
18. **das Einrad** (dahs **ighn**-raht)   unicycle
19. **das Drahtseil** (dahs **dRaht**-zighl)   tightrope
20. **das Sicherheitsnetz** (dahs **ziH**-aiR-hights-nets)   safety net
21. **die Seilleiter** (dee **zighl**-ligh-taiR)   rope ladder
22. **der Zeremonienmeister** (daiR tsaiR-Re-moh-**nee**-en-migh-staiR)
    master of ceremonies
23. **die Stange** (dee **shtahng**-guh)   pole
24. **das Trapez** (dahs trahp-**payts**)   trapeze
25. **der Trapezkünstler** (daiR trahp-**payts**-keunst-laiR)   trapeze artist

Fragen   (Questions)

1. Who is going through "der Feuerring"?
2. What is the boy in the audience eating?
3. What is the tightrope walker riding?
4. What object does the trainer have in his hand?

20. Die Musikinstrumente
   (dee **moo**-zik-in-stRoo-**ment**-tuh)
   Musical Instruments

1. **die Gitarre** (dee gee-**tahR**-Ruh) guitar
2. **die Maracas** (dee mah-**Rah**-kahs) maracas
3. **die Kesselpauke** (dee **kes**-sel-pow-kuh) kettledrum
4. **die Kastagnetten** (dee kahst-tahn-**yet**-ten) castanets
5. **die Trompete** (dee tRom-**pay**-tuh) trumpet
6. **das Tamburin** (dahs tahm-booR-**Reen**) tambourine

7. **die Geige** (dee **gigh**-guh) violin
8. **der Kontrabaß** (daiR **kon**-tRah-bahs) bass
9. **die Mandoline** (dee mahn-doh-**lee**-nuh) mandolin
10. **der Bariton** (daiR bah-Ri-**tohn**) baritone
11. **die Harfe** (dee **hahR**-fuh) harp
12. **das Banjo** (dahs **bahn**-joh) banjo
13. **das Saxophon** (dahs **zahks**-oh-fohn) saxophone
14. **die Klarinette** (dee klahR-Ri-**net**-tuh) clarinet
15. **das Klavier** (dahs klah-**veeR**) piano
16. **die Posaune** (dee poh-**zown**-nuh) trombone

Fragen (Questions)

1. Name six instruments with strings.
2. Name five wind instruments.
3. What is "die Kesselpauke"?
4. Name an instrument that has a keyboard.

21. Die Tätigkeitswörter (dee **tayt**-tig-kights-**vOER**-taiR)
Action Words

1. **schaukeln** (**show**-keln) to swing
2. **schreiben** (**shRigh**-ben) to write
3. **tanzen** (**tahn**-tsen) to dance
4. **essen** (**es**-sen) to eat
5. **träumen** (**tRoy**-men) to dream
6. **zeichnen** (**tsighH**-nen) to draw

schreiben

7. **spielen** (**shpee**-len) to play
8. **arbeiten** (**ahR**-bigh-ten) to work
9. **Rollschuh laufen** (**rohl**-shoo lowf-fen) to (roller) skate
10. **Fahrrad fahren** (**fahR**-Raht **fahR**-Ren) to ride a bicycle
11. **ausstrecken** (**ows**-strek-ken) to stretch

Fragen (Questions)

1. What do you do before you play a sport?
2. What do you do with a pencil?
3. What do you do with skates?
4. What is "tanzen"?

22. Die Zahlen (dee tsah-len)   Numbers

1. **eins** (ighns)   one
2. **zwei** (tsvigh)   two
3. **drei** (dRigh)   three
4. **vier** (feeR)   four
5. **fünf** (feunf)   five
6. **sechs** (zeks)   six
7. **sieben** (zee-ben)   seven
8. **acht** (ahKt)   eight
9. **neun** (noyn)   nine
10. **zehn** (tsayn)   ten

Fragen   (Questions)

1. How many strawberries are there in the picture?
2. How many lemons are there in the picture?
3. How many flowers do you see in the picture?
4. How many peaches do you see?

23. Die Formen (dee **fohR**-men)   Shapes

1. **das Viereck** (dahs **feeR**-ek)   square
2. **der Rhombus** (daiR **Rohm**-boos)   rhombus
3. **der Stern** (daiR shtaiRn)   star
4. **das Oval** (dahs **oh**-vahl)   oval
5. **das Dreieck** (dahs **dry**-ek)   triangle
6. **der Kreis** (daiR kRighs)   circle
7. **das Rechteck** (dahs **ReH**-tek)   rectangle
8. **der Halbmond** (daiR **halp**-mohnt)   crescent

Fragen   (Questions)

1. Name three shapes that have four sides.
2. Name one shape that has three sides.
3. Which shape looks like a star?
4. What is "der Kreis"?

Antworten auf die Fragen / Answers to the Questions

1. Unser Haus

1. the garden hose
2. die Forke, die Blumenkelle
3. die Mauer, der Holzzaun
4. der Gärtner

2. Das Wohnzimmer

1. die Stricknadeln
2. der Enkel
3. die Uhr
4. das Buch

3. Die Küche

1. der Rostbraten
2. das Wasser
3. der Toast
4. der Lappen

4. Das Klassenzimmer

1. die Schere
2. die Subtraktion, die Vervielfachung, die Addition
3. der Arbeitskittel
4. der Dinosaurier, die Uhr, das Photo, der Kalender

5. Die Kleidung

1. die Brille
2. der Pyjama
3. die Socken
4. der Badeanzug

6. Die Jahreszeiten und das Wetter

1. der Regenbogen
2. der Sommer
3. der Blitz, der Regen
4. der Mond

7. Der Sport

1. das Baseballspiel
2. das Skifahren
3. das Radfahren
4. das Kegeln

8. Die Stadt

1. der Unfall
2. der Krankenwagen
3. der Polizist
4. the traffic lights

9. Der Supermarkt

1. das Eis
2. die Kirschen, die Kartoffeln, die Karotten, die Kohle
3. die Kassiererin
4. der Verkäufer

10. Im Restaurant

1. der Küchenchef
2. die Kellnerin
3. das belegte Brot
4. die Speisekarte

11. Das Postamt

1. das Postamt, der Briefkasten
2. die Adresse, die Briefmarke
3. der Briefträger
4. the newspaper

12. Die Bank

1. die Bank, der Tresor, das Bankfach
2. der Tresor
3. die Wache
4. das Einzahlungsformular

13. Beim Arzt

1. das Stethoskop
2. der Tierarzt
3. die Krankenschwester
4. the bandage

14. Die Tankstelle

1. der Mechaniker
2. the gas pump
3. der Abschleppwagen
4. die Autowaschanlage

15. Die Verkehrsmittel

1. der Fallschirm
2. das Fahrrad, das Motorrad
3. das Unterseeboot
4. die Rakete

16. Der Bauernhof

1. die Bäuerin
2. der Stall, das Korral
3. der Bulle, das Pferd, die Kuh,
   das Schaf, der Truthahn, die Gans,
   das Schwein, das Huhn, die Ziege
4. der Schweinestall

17. Die Tiere im Zoo

1. die Giraffe
2. der Eisbär
3. der Papagei, der Quetzal
4. das Reh

18. Am Strand

1. der Sonnenschirm
2. die Sandburg
3. das Pferd, die Seemöwe, die Robbe,
   die Muschel
4. die Insel

19. Der Zirkus

1. der Tiger
2. die Zuckerwatte
3. das Einrad
4. die Peitsche

20. Die Musikinstrumente

1. die Gitarre, das Banjo, die Harfe,
   die Geige, der Kontrabaß,
   die Mandoline
2. die Trompete, das Saxophon, die
   Posaune, die Klarinette, der Bariton
3. the kettledrum
4. das Klavier

21. Die Tätigkeitswörter

1. ausstrecken
2. schreiben, zeichnen
3. Rollschuh laufen
4. to dance

22. Die Zahlen

1. zwei
2. acht
3. drei
4. sechs

23. Die Formen

1. das Viereck, das Rechteck,
   der Rhombus
2. das Dreieck
3. der Stern
4. a circle